ME, HER & THEM

Humours and Tremors

"...life without spice is like scotch without ice..."

– a husband unknown

By
Arnab Biswas

*This book is dedicated to
all urban couples
around the world.*

CONTENTS

ANIKET'S MONOLOGUE

We Indians, take marriage quite seriously.

It is a lifelong commitment between two individuals. Many believe it marks the beginning of a lifelong relationship between two families.

Our Bollywood movies have inspired this dream, often portraying families coming together to celebrate this journey.

The nature of celebrations reflects the traditions and culture of the families.

In this era of globalization, marriages have become even more exciting. Marriages are taking place across diverse geographies, cultures, creeds, and religions.

Rituals and customs are beautifully fused to celebrate this blend of cultures. Bachelor and bachelorette parties, destination weddings, wedding planners, themed décor, photo props, and behind-the-scenes shoots are all the rage these days.

While the scale of celebrations may vary across different economic backgrounds, the joy and enjoyment of the occasion remain universal.

I too experienced this rite of passage. I was fortunate to marry the person I was head over heels in love with.

She was special. I use 'was' here, only to underscore the difference in the way I looked at her before marriage.

Her eye-catching beauty and glamour mixed with her sharp intellect made me fall for her from the moment we met.

Her professional success at a very young age, along with all the said qualities, made her someone I wanted to be with.

One may call me out for being superficial. But in my defense, I would say that I am a 'Man'.

One fine day, I gathered my courage to tell her how I felt about her. Unfortunately, rejection was her first response.

I was not let down by it, she was too special to let go of and that too just because of one rejection. I pursued her for months and years.

Finally, that day came. She agreed, breaking the norms of her conservative Tamil family.

A 'Vegetarian Tamil' girl came forward to accept a 'Fish loving Bengali' boy as her life partner.

It was my dream come true. I felt myself becoming more responsible. I did not want to miss a single opportunity to be with her.

Just to get a glimpse of her, I would brave the chaotic traffic of Chennai for what felt like ages.

Even on weekends, I'd wake at dawn to drop her off at the gym—those 15 minutes together made my hour-long drive worthwhile.

Her usual slow reply to my messages were the most anxious moments of my life. I was filled with a sense of insecurity.

"What if…?" The unwanted scenarios conjured up by my imagination kept my nerves perpetually tense. Only the 'Ting' of a notification, accompanied by a preview of her message flashing on my screen, could put my mind at ease.

"Did her parents take her to meet a boy's family? Did she find someone better than me?" Countless such hypothetical questions transformed me—a person once known for his carefree personality—into a paranoid wreck.

Those emotions, those excitements, became part of me, and were my motivation.

Then it happened—we got married. And from then on, it felt different.

What was once an aspiration had now become a reality. There would be no more chases, no more thrilling uncertainty. The anxious moments would now be replaced by the predictable mundane rhythm of daily life.

I felt a significant void inside me.

"What now?" I wondered.

But then, the universe works in its own ways. It answered my question. It set off a series of events as soon as we got married.

Just when I thought our marriage was the final episode, a brand-new season was released.

Each episode has been packed with action, drama, romance and suspense. There is no dearth of anxious moments.

I like to call this series, 'Humours and Tremors'.

Marriage didn't mark the end of the spice in my life; it simply changed its flavour.

What follows are glimpses into this journey—15 years and counting.

೫೦೦೫

THE PRINCESS, THE CASTLE
AND A FISH-EATING OGRE

A few months into our relationship, I was transferred to Gurgaon. Priya did not want to let this forced distance complicate our relationship. She started negotiations with her employer. She soon followed.

Being away from the rules and restrictions of Priya's conservative family, we discovered a carefree new life together.

We began to understand each other at a deeper level. The seriousness of our relationship took a quantum leap.

"Appa is coming to meet you," Priya informed me on a chilly winter day, just as I reached for a biscuit to dip in my tea.

I knew Priya had mentioned our relationship to her family, but I wasn't completely aware of their reaction.

"Oh! Sure!" I wheezed, inadvertently dropping the biscuit into my cup. The winter chill masked my shaky voice as I nervously watched the once firm biscuit slowly dissolve in the tea, feeling the weight of the impending encounter loom over me.

"Trust me, this isn't going to be easy," Priya cautioned me.

"Don't worry, dear, I know how to make an impression," I said, trying my best to put up a brave face. Only I knew how fast my heart was thumping.

"Oh, really! We'll see." Priya took me literally, being totally oblivious to my inner emotions.

"I can help!" Priya made a last-ditch effort to shield me from an impending disaster.

"The only help I need from you is to never leave my side. I can handle the rest," I replied, determined not to show any sign of weakness.

"Okay, then…" Priya shifted to another topic.

I started to prepare. I crafted a comprehensive resume in my mind that highlighted all my positive qualities, showcasing why I would be an ideal match for Priya as her potential husband.

I was confident in defending my own case. Priya just played along.

***

Finally, the day arrived—or rather, the evening. I had crossed every T and dotted all the I's to ensure I would leave a lasting positive impression on him.

Dressed in a white sweater and my favourite pair of jeans, I arrived at the coffee shop of the Marriott hotel.

There he was, sitting at the table I had pre-booked. A man in his mid-50s, wearing glasses.

I glanced at my phone. I was five minutes late. So much for making a good impression.

"Hello," he greeted, extending his hand as I walked up to him.

As he stood up to greet me, I got a closer look at him. He was nearly my height and had a head full of grey hair. A big smile spread across his face.

"Maybe this is a sign of affirmation and acceptance," I thought to myself, feeling my nerves begin to settle.

After mentally reviewing my well-prepared resume, I found a sense of confidence washing over me. "I can do this!"

"Do you want some tea?" he asked politely.

I nodded. He called the waiter. He went through all the options. A pot of Earl Grey was ordered.

"I am generally a coffee drinker. But you guys don't seem to have good filter coffee here," his first comment to me as he settled back on to the sofa.

I did not know how to address that complaint, so I just smiled in response.

Then for a while we talked about the serious flight delays at Delhi Airport caused by the fog. We swapped a few anecdotes and shared a few laughs over that.

I began to feel at ease with him.

"Here is your tea sir!" the waiter interrupted.

As a gesture of politeness, I poured tea into both our cups.

Appa took a long sip and closed his eyes. It was as if he was gathering his thoughts before jumping into the main topic of our discussion.

"Let me share our background and my thoughts," after a brief pause, he broke his silence.

I was all ears. It felt like my early days in college when I had the habit of jotting down every single word my professors uttered.

"I'd classify things into four buckets," he continued. With his hand gestures, it was easy for me to picture four imaginary buckets sitting between us.

Like a reality show host, he was about to open each of them one by one and I was about to get rated.

"Bucket One- me and my family background." He opened the first bucket.

For the next thirty minutes, he took me on a journey through the cultural heritage of his family. It felt like flipping through a chapter of a history book.

Generations of academic, professional, and financial successes were something truly worth celebrating.

He emphasized how he was the first-generation liberal in his family, embracing the changes of the modern world.

When he recounted standing up to his relatives for his son's association with a girl from Himachal, a proud expression lit up his face.

Seeing him so proud of that moment, I gave him a smile with hearts in my eyes.

His subtle yet affirmative stance on cross-cultural marriages encouraged me.

I started to imagine a scene where Priya and I were at Delhi Airport giving him a warm sendoff together.

"Priya is my beloved daughter. She means a lot to me," he said as he opened the second bucket.

As he started to talk more and more about Priya, his voice began to tremble, full of emotion. Soon, he was choking up.

If the first bucket had felt like a chapter from a history book, this one was more like a carefully preserved album of Priya's life.

We turned the pages together, her childhood days, her academic brilliance, her professional achievements, and countless other milestones.

Finally, he concluded by reflecting on how her upbringing overseas had made it natural for her to get attracted to cross cultural relationships.

By the time we reached the bottom of bucket two, his eyes were moist.

I found myself imagining the moment on the wedding day when the father hands over his daughter to the groom.

I could sense us connecting to each other through our emotions for Priya.

In the meantime, the waiter arrived with another pot of tea. We sipped our tea in silence. The emotions that had reached a high, needed to settle down.

After a while, he opened the third bucket.

"For Priya, I would always respect her choice." He took a pause and then continued. "But I do have some conditions."

"Here come the terms and conditions," I was all set to press the accept button.

Agreeing to terms and conditions has become an inherent part of survival. In this modern age, there's no escaping it.

We all know T&Cs operate on a one-way street. If you want something, you must accept the accompanying terms, whether you like them or not.

The rejection or disagreement buttons are mere trickery. If you choose to reject, you in turn will be rejected.

"Marriage is not just between the boy and the girl; it is also a union between two families," he continued...

"Shall I fix a date with my parents for a meeting?" I asked politely, signalling my intent to press the accept button.

To my disappointment, my words didn't quite register with him.

"You are a Bengali and a non-vegetarian," he stated, putting me on the spot.

"See, you and she can't even share a meal together," he continued, his tone becoming more critical.

"But! But…" I stammered, struggling to gather my thoughts.

"Poor her! If I agree to this, she'll have to hide in a corner and eat her meals alone," he said, his tone growing increasingly negative.

"Priya, all by herself, surrounded by people with no similarity to her." He went on…

"People? Corner?" I was struggling to visualize these points. It's going to be just Priya and me. And we would only have to deal with either two ends of the sofa or two sides of the dining table. Where would these people and the corner even come from?

Besides, Bengali cuisine has a huge spread of vegetarian delicacies. I was all set for a counter argument.

"You heard me this far. Would you disagree with anything I've said?" he asked.

It was my turn to respond, but suddenly it struck me.

It was a trick question. If I disagreed and put forward my own points, I would be viewed as a disrespectful and argumentative person, and hence rejected.

If I agreed, then I was already rejected.

I chose a middle path. "Yes, I agree there are some differences, but Priya and I can work those out," I said in an effort to allay his concern.

"You know, girls' parents think very differently from boys' parents," he replied with a meaningful smile. I could see that he was smartly disassociating himself from his earlier avatar of openness to a cross-cultural alliance.

The message was clear. What he accepted as a son's father, he was rejecting as a daughter's father.

This, I guessed, was his fourth bucket. My heart sank.

"I wish Priya were here to stand up for us," I thought helplessly.

I had never felt so unprepared. I was ready to present my case based on my family background, academic achievements, career prospects, and above all, my love for Priya.

But food preferences and cultural differences? I hadn't anticipated those as criteria for our relationship. I should not have turned down Priya's offer for help.

"Then, let me summarize," his concluding remark breaking my train of thought.

His summary was perfect and accurate, but it only reflected his perspective. It completely omitted the one line I had managed to get in.

Just then, his phone rang. "Oh, I need to go, Priya is here," he said, glancing at his phone and jumping up. He called the waiter to settle the bill.

"It's okay, uncle, you carry on; I'll take care of it," I needed some time to myself to clear my head.

"Okay then, bye!" he said, walking away.

I ordered a drink and sat there, trying to make sense of what had just happened.

It took me some time to process it all.

As the first shot of single malt warmed me up, a sense of clarity started to settle in.

I started to appreciate the story he had just told me.

First, he had shared the glorified legacy of his family, painting a picture of his castle. Then, with an emotional recount of Priya's life, he described the princess. In this story, I was nothing more than a simple fish-eating ogre.

He made it abundantly clear that the ogre had no place in a princess's tale. While Priya may have been a free princess, as the king and knight of the castle, he would take the final call, according to his wishes.

I dialled Priya's number, but she disconnected the call. A message came through a little later.

"Don't worry...I am still by your side...told you, you needed help... pick me up in the morning :-)"

Despite the king's rejection, my princess's warm message brought my smile back.

I called the waiter over, settled the bill and headed home.

ഇൗരു

TWO MATCHES IN ONE DAY

'm quite experienced in weddings—oops, I mean attending them. I've been to so many.

The vibrations of Sanskrit mantras, the tune of the shehnai, the intoxicating smells of food, flowers, and perfumes, and the eye-catching bright colours—they're all familiar to me.

But my own wedding stands out in my memory, filled with the hooting, whistling, cheering, and dancing that accompanied the rituals.

At the very beginning of this narration I must emphasize that we got married only after Priya's parents approved of the match.

Priya's persistence lasted for about five years—far longer than the duration of a test match. She eventually convinced the King and the Knight to say Yes. Throughout this time, I stood by her side, as a source of motivation.

Our perseverance paid off, bringing our parents together to plan every detail of the wedding. The agreement was to conduct the ceremony following traditional Tamil rituals.

At first, my parents felt a bit uncomfortable with the long procedures that Tamil rituals are known for. However, an abridged version was soon worked out to ease the concerns and close the negotiation.

But I had a different concern.

"That means we have to get married in the morning?" I asked Priya.

Bengalis get wed in the evening. My entire life has been oriented in that way. Late to bed, late to rise.

"Obviously! What's wrong with that? You should be happy Appa and Amma finally agreed," she replied, leaving no room for negotiation.

I had to fall in line.

Then began the process of finalization of the date. It was like a quest for an optimal point on a multi-dimensional plane.

The quest began with matching planetary alignments with our horoscopes.

And then came the feasibility of friends and family's attendance, managing conflicts with already planned marriages in the extended family and finally, the availability of wedding venues.

A couple of days before the big day, my parents led a delegation from Kolkata to Chennai of around 100 people, friends and relatives. A grand welcome awaited them at Chennai Airport.

A warmup session was arranged in style on the eve of the wedding to help the families warm up to each other.

The event was held in the party hall of a five-star hotel. It featured exotic food, karaoke, DJ and dance floor–catalysts to make the evening an unforgettable one.

The evening started with a music reality show-style event, where a few participants were so enthusiastic that they were unwilling to leave the stage for others.

Sensing the situation might get a bit complicated, someone turned off the lights, and the DJ took charge.

Everyone hit the dance floor to shake a leg, the thumping music proving intoxicating for young and old alike.

In that moment, a wave of euphoria washed over me. I surrendered to the rhythm and the beat, losing track of everything around me.

I felt the impact of it all the next morning.

"Good morning, dear! Wake up, it's our special day today!" Priya's loving voice pulled me from my sleep. It was 5 AM.

I felt like a zombie, my head pounding as hazy images of a bar and drinks flowing flashed through my mind. I couldn't quite remember how I'd ended up there.

"Hello? Are you there?" her anxious voice broke through my foggy recollection.

"Yeah, yeah… don't worry, I'm up," I reassured her, while desperate for a few more minutes of sleep.

"What time is the wedding again?" I asked hesitantly.

"Just get ready and come over," she said, her tone firm.

The call ended abruptly. I set my alarm for 5:15 and closed my eyes for a quick power nap.

Just then…

"Ani… get up! You're going to be late!" My mother was banging on the door, urgency in her voice.

"Yes, yes, I'm up," I moaned as I lazily opened the door.

She was already dressed to the nines. I couldn't believe someone could look so put together at sunrise.

By around 6:30, we arrived at the hotel where our wedding was to take place.

"Sir, this way," a gentleman in a black suit welcomed us with a smooth voice. He guided us to the wedding hall.

Vijay, Priya's brother, was waiting there to welcome us. "Welcome, my friend. Don't let the large crowd intimidate you today," he said with a big smile, shaking my hand.

"I don't get intimidated so easily, buddy. I'm quite used to dealing with crowds in the hundreds at our office events," I shook it off.

"Hundreds, huh? Well, let's see," Vijay gave a knowing smile and led us into the hall.

"Please make yourselves comfortable. I'll go and check on Priya," he said, settling us on a sofa placed at the back of the hall before he walked away.

My parents started to check out the hall.

The stage was set for the big event, with two giant screens perfectly placed on either side. It looked like people had worked tirelessly to get everything ready. My parents looked impressed.

"I like the grandeur. Aniket totally deserves this," Ma said, smiling.

"Cool! You'll be on the big screen!" Baba exclaimed; his excitement palpable.

"All this looks good, but why are there so many chairs?" Ma asked. Her curious eyes were measuring every inch of the hall.

"How many chairs are there?" Baba went along. Ma's general curiosity about things was not unfamiliar to him.

"At least two thousand!" she replied, looking stunned.

"We brought only a hundred people. If only I'd known... there are so many we did not bring here!" she lamented.

As they continued listing out all the guests they could have brought along, I felt the need to do something about my throbbing headache.

My head was still pounding from the hangover, each throb a reminder of the night before. I did not want to take any medicine as I was sure Priya wouldn't appreciate a drowsy groom.

I pushed through it and grabbed a bottle of water, chugging it down desperately. I kept reaching for more until my bladder finally rebelled.

"Let me make a quick visit to the loo," I told Ma. By then the Kolkata gang had started to arrive and both my parents got busy with them.

I wish I had the time to check if they were making a roll call. A mere hundred people can easily get lost in the ocean of two thousand. I was sure Ma was doing her best to keep her small Bengali gang together.

After the relief, it took me a little longer to re-adjust the dhoti. I hurried back to the hall.

It was a shocker. The hall was jam-packed. Was I in the right hall?

Just then, I felt a tap on my shoulder, it was Vijay.

"What are you doing here? It's your wedding, no? Come on, everyone's waiting!" he said sarcastically.

Before I could assess the situation in totality, Vijay rushed me to the stage.

Priya was already there, flanked by her parents, the priest, and my cousin sister. When she looked up, I felt her gaze pierce through me—a stare that could take me to the stairs of hell.

Was I still reeking of alcohol from last night? Was it my delay that had kept her waiting? Or was it my zombie-like response to her earlier wake-up call? I couldn't help but wonder what had provoked that look.

With no chance to explain myself, I resolved to show my sincerity and devotion. I focused intently on the rituals, determined to give them my undivided attention.

The four-hour ritual began. The priest chanted mantras in Sanskrit, followed by English translations, line by line.

As the ceremony unfolded, I felt a wave of excitement wash over me, we were finally getting married!

A montage of our last five years together played in my mind.

About fifteen minutes in, I sensed a ripple of energy coursing through the hall. It was the collective excitement of the audience.

The happy buzz made me smile, but I kept my focus on the rituals.

Moments later, the crowd erupted into applause, adding to the joyful atmosphere.

Curiosity bubbled up inside me, and I was tempted to look around to see what was causing the applause. But Priya was watching me closely, and the fear of agitating her further kept me fully focused on the rituals.

As time passed, the clapping and cheering grew louder, reaching a crescendo. By the end of the ceremony, I could hear people hooting and whistling.

I had no idea that people in Chennai were such marriage enthusiasts. The electrifying cheers and applause felt like a standing ovation for a stage performer.

I had never witnessed such joyful reactions to a wedding ceremony before. Rather I have seen people tend to skip the ceremony and participate more in the pre-wedding bash and post-wedding buffet.

Although, I felt grateful to the crowd.

Without their enthusiastic responses, I might not have been able to endure the four-hour long ceremony.

The fear of Priya's stare kept me focused but it was the audience's energy that truly motivated me to stay engaged.

Finally, the rituals came to a close. The priest declared us as husband and wife.

The crowd erupted into dancing and whistling.

As Priya and I came down from the stage, I leaned in and whispered to her, "We're so fortunate—our marriage rituals were performed in front of such a large energetic crowd."

"What are you talking about?" she snapped back,

"I'm sorry!" I apologized, in my effort to cool her down.

"Look how nice everyone is! They've been cheering and hooting throughout the ceremony," I tried to lighten her mood, gesturing toward the ocean of two thousand smiling faces in the crowd.

"Ani, please turn around and look," she said, pointing at one of the giant screens.

"What is that?" I gasped in shock. It was a cricket stadium, and the Indian players were celebrating.

"Oh, today was the T20 final. Damn! I missed the match!" I blurted out and immediately faced the consequences.

"You all are the same. God knows why I made so much effort to make this day happen!" Priya's face turned red.

"All went well, didn't it!" Appa's cheerful entry saved me from further scolding from Priya.

"Jesus! The crowd went crazy. I was absolutely on target," his grin growing wider.

"See, it's not me, it's your father," I whispered to Priya.

"I managed two overlapping matches flawlessly," his excitement was overflowing.

"Two matches?" I was dumbfounded. I looked at Priya.

"I understand the T-20 match, which one is the other one?" Missing one match was already painful, but missing two was unacceptable.

"The other one is our match. The bride and the groom. Wake up!" Priya was clearly annoyed.

Before I could even begin damage control…

"What a moment! Finally, India won an ICC final!" Vijay joined in.

And then came the explosion.

"So, our wedding was of no importance!" Priya was furious.

She was so loud that her words reached every corner of the hall. The crowd fell silent.

"Let's go and grab lunch, let them enjoy their cricket match. I don't want to be here another minute," said Priya, dragging me by the arm to the buffet.

I found an opportunity.

"Come what may, our match will always stand out. Our match is made in heaven and not in a cricket stadium. Thank you for becoming my wife!" I whispered in her ear.

"Yes, finally our long wait is over. I love you," she whispered back, burying her face in my chest. A tight hug followed.

As we walked towards the buffet, the cheers from the crowd resumed in the background.

I couldn't help but wonder- which match were they cheering for now?

ღოღ

THE CULTURAL CONUNDRUM

thought that with the wedding reception complete, Priya and I could finally wrap things up and return to our easygoing, carefree lives.

Perhaps it's the salesperson in me—once the deal is sealed, the contract signed, and the deliverables checked off, the job feels done.

But what I overlooked was the real, ongoing work, Relationship Management.

In the corporate world, these tasks are neatly divided among different departments, but in marriage, you're the whole team. There's no handoff; you have to embrace the DIY approach.

After our time in Chennai, it was Kolkata's turn—the City of Joy.

Amongst our friends and family, word had spread, Aniket had married a South Indian girl.

Initially, Priya and I were indeed joyful, as family, neighbours and friends streamed in to see my South Indian wife.

On one such day, a very close group of relatives visited us.

"So, you're South Indian?" one of my aunts asked Priya.

"I'm from the southern part of India, yes—I'm Tamil," Priya replied, though her smile faded slightly.

"But you're so fair!" another aunt chimed in, clearly surprised.

Priya looked a bit uncomfortable.

My mother, sensing the moment, quickly offered, "She was born and raised overseas."

Listening to this exchange, I found myself wondering how any of these things are connected.

To date I am still trying hard to trace these seemingly well understood links between geography, upbringing and skin colour.

"I am quite familiar with your culture. I've spent some time down there," one of my many uncles broke into my thoughts with this profound declaration.

"Oh really! Which part of Chennai?" Priya asked, her curiosity piqued.

"Oh no, not Chennai," my uncle corrected quickly. "I was in Hyderabad for a while."

"Oh," Priya said, taken aback.

As the conversation meandered, one of my mom's friends leaned in to add her own vision of our future life,

"You two can relax and enjoy now. After all, all Priya needs to cook at home is dosa and idli. You'll have so much time for other things!"

"I wish we had it that easy," Ma's friend continued with a sigh. "Our cooking never ends! Every day, we have to make something new, and at least three or four dishes per meal."

"Yes," Ma joined in with a laugh.

"Our day has four stages; we cook, we feed, we eat, we sleep. There's no time for anything else." She made her point.

I couldn't help but wonder why she left out the TV time. Soaps were undeniably an integral part of her life. But before I could bring it up, Priya spoke up.

"You know, we eat more than just idli and dosa."

The room suddenly fell quiet.

The idea of 'South Indian food' beyond idli and dosa seemed to stun our Bengali friends and family.

"Yes, we have a whole variety of Tamil dishes," Priya added. "And we enjoy Italian, Chinese, and everything else too."

A quiet surprise settled over the room as everyone processed this unexpected expansion of 'South Indian' cuisine. All their traditional wisdom was, for the moment, overturned.

"Priya, you should share some of these recipes with everyone," my mother suggested, trying to lighten the moment.

I could see trouble brewing. Priya didn't cook.

"Enough about food—let's talk about something else…" I quickly interjected, steering the conversation away before Priya could reveal this fact.

Without me stepping in, she might have blurted it out, and that would've become a topic for endless family discussions!

My mother didn't know how to cook when she got married, so I was well aware of what revealing Priya's secret might lead to.

Whispers and gossip, as though some long-buried scandal had resurfaced.

Even now, more than 35 years into her marriage, despite feeding countless friends and family delicious meals made by herself, my mother still hears about her 'culinary deficiency' from her early days.

She was just 21—for God's sake!

***

After countless such visits and rounds of small talk, the 'City of Joy' began to feel a bit less joyful for Priya and me.

We escaped to Africa, craving the solace of nature and the company of beings who, thankfully, don't pass judgment. At least so far, the wildlife remains blissfully free of opinions and unsolicited advice.

I wish I could end this story on that happy note. But that was not meant to be.

We had to return to Chennai to complete the loop of post-marriage relationship management on Priya's side.

Without delving into too many details, let's just say I had my work cut out for me in establishing my identity as more than just a North Indian, an admirer of Tagore, and a 'fish and rice eater.'

ೠ

A SILLY TANTRUM

A few months into our marriage, I got an overseas posting. Marriage seemed to have brought me a new streak of luck.

With the work permit and visa sorted, Priya and I were gearing up for a fresh start. We were ready to become expats.

Admiration and adulation, mixed with a hint of jealousy, spread among my colleagues.

Overnight, my LinkedIn network grew substantially, and Facebook was not far behind. I could feel a sudden desire among many to get to know me.

However, some savvy individuals took a more traditional approach by reaching out to my wife with their best wishes and goodwill. After all, her connection with me is more real than social network platforms.

Then came the final step. My colleagues organized a farewell party for me.

As the day approached, I started to feel the excitement. The event was set to take place at a luxury hotel, complete with unlimited free food and drinks—especially my favorite, single malt whisky. It was about to be a perfect send-off.

But there was something that bothered me. Priya was becoming increasingly secretive. Calls from some unknown number would lead her to a corner of the house, where I couldn't hear or see her.

I started to notice it after a showdown between Priya and me. Our first ever.

It was the day she suddenly took quite an interest in upgrading my appearance for my new job.

"You'll be part of the Country Leadership team now," she began.

I nodded absentmindedly, focused on replying to work emails.

"You should start wearing a wristwatch, especially one with a metal band. It would go well with your suits," she added.

That was where she broke through my distraction. This is where I needed to respond to Priya.

"In a world with smartphones, who even wears a wristwatch anymore?" I snapped. "I expected better from you."

"A leather band, maybe. But metal? Out of the question!" the intensity of my rejection of her idea increased.

"You really…" I went on…

Priya looked a little sad. It must have been tough for her to see me disagree with her for the first time.

After that, the secret calls started.

***

Then the day came- the day of my farewell party.

Priya dressed in her usual classy style, while I was in jeans and a T-shirt.

It was quite the party. First, my frenemies and colleagues reminisced about our good times together at work, and then Priya said a few words.

She mostly spoke about my lazy and easygoing personality outside of work. I noticed many curious eyes glued on her—perhaps this was their first and only chance to visualize me as a couch potato.

Drinks, dinner, and dancing followed. As the sweat started to mix with the scent of our imported perfumes, it was time to say goodbye.

The goodbye moment became even more special when they approached me with a gift.

I was genuinely touched by their thoughtfulness. They didn't just pick a gift, they had carefully prepared two options, allowing me the privilege of selecting the one I liked best.

After a few last-minute hugs and handshakes, Priya and I finally got into our car.

As the driver started the engine, I noticed something was off. Priya was grumpy.

The discomfort I had been feeling for the past few days returned.

Even in my intoxicated state, I made an effort to analyze what could have gone wrong.

"Is she still upset about our earlier disagreement?" I wondered.

"Or was it something I did today at the party?" The possibilities started to expand in my mind.

I avoided asking her such private questions in the presence of our driver.

As the single malt coursed through my bloodstream, I found myself slowly losing my ability to do any further analysis. I dozed off.

The next thing I remember is waking up with a searing headache. It was nearly noon.

As I dragged myself to the bathroom, fragments of the previous night started flooding back. A splash of cold water on my face made me feel a little better.

"Oh no! Priya is upset, I need to go and find her!" I rushed out of the bathroom.

She was sitting on the living room sofa, surrounded by piles of her clothes and belongings. She was packing.

The dark circles under her eyes indicated she hadn't gotten much sleep, and she still looked grumpy.

"What is she doing? It can't be…" I was in a state of panic, my mind was racing.

Thanks to seventies movies, I knew that when a wife starts packing, it's never good news for the husband.

"Is she going back to her parents' house?"

Scary thoughts flooded my mind. I walked up to her. I noticed her teary eyes.

"How could you?" Her words struck me like splinters from an explosion.

What started as silent sobs soon turned into full-blown howling.

I tried to comfort her, but she pushed me away.

"You embarrassed me in front of the whole world," she cried.

"What did I do wrong?" I was like a forlorn dog in a cartoon, with ears flattened and tail tucked between my legs.

"You completely embarrassed me," she repeated, tears streaming down her big, expressive eyes. It felt like the ground was shaking beneath me, as if I were being buried alive.

"I'm sorry," I said, my voice filled with desperation. I just wanted her to stop crying, even though I had no idea what I was apologizing for.

"You're so damn unpredictable; I don't know who you really are," she sobbed.

"Please, babe, tell me what I did wrong. I promise I'll never do it again. I love you so much," I said, desperate to restore some normalcy to this moment of gloom and stress.

After a while of cajoling, she finally settled down. Her tears stopped, and she began to narrate the whole incident. I listened intently, eager to understand.

"That day, you gave me an hour-long rundown on why metal band watches aren't your thing—they're heavy, clunky, and just not your style!" she paused.

I clearly remembered this incident. I was more anxious to know what was coming next.

"Your team was in a mess and all because of me. They originally bought a metal watch for you, and they wanted me to check with you," she continued.

"Ah, that's why you were going on about the metal watch?" I asked.

"Obviously, why else? I gave up on your fashion sense a long time ago," she sounded resigned.

"I relayed your comments to them, but your favourite Shashi, wasn't convinced," she continued.

"I don't even remember how many calls I had to take for that. It wasn't fun at all," her frustration was clear.

"Shashi kept arguing, as if I was guiding them wrong," Priya said, visibly agitated.

"It turned out that Shashi and I were holding up the process. Thankfully, Rajat saved the day. He suggested presenting both options, a leather watch and a metal one, and letting you decide there," Priya sighed.

"Oh! I see now," I said, finally understanding what had actually gone wrong. Thankfully, it was nothing more than bruising Priya's ego.

"But what's the point of all this? You suddenly decided to go with the metal watch. You should've seen the victorious smirk on Shashi's face," she sounded jealous.

She stood up to get me a set of fresh towels. I guess the outburst finally cleared the cloud in her mind.

"Please, go take a shower. You look miserable," she said with an innocent smile lighting up the room. Her smile after her tears, felt like a new rainbow after a cloud burst.

I wanted to make it up to her. I pulled her towards me, gently taking her hand. I dropped to one knee.

A shy smile spread across her face, a soft pink hue colouring her cheeks.

"What are you doing?" her voice was husky and choked with emotion.

"I will always be by your side, for better or worse", I said with sincerity. Our eyes locked.

"I'll always endure your tantrums, however silly they are," I added, making a solemn promise... and then...

Bang! Priya pushed me away and locked herself in our bedroom. I was left stranded—no shower, followed by a day of prolonged starvation.

ॐ

THE SHORT-LIVED SUPREMACY

Finally, the day arrived when Priya and I landed in K-land, my expat job location. Before our final move, I had the privilege of visiting for a week to do house hunting.

I settled upon a two-bedroom villa, fully furnished. It was nestled among several foreign embassies, with stunning views from the balcony. There were high mountains on one side and a river on the other.

Priya and I took a pre-arranged cab from the airport and headed straight to our new home.

Priya devoted herself to setting up our new home while I focused on familiarizing myself with my new job. Together, we began exploring the city whenever we had some free time.

It took us about a month to settle in.

We were enjoying the convenience of a developed nation to the fullest. But there was one challenge. We were unable to find a cook who could make Indian dishes.

A month passed, and we managed to get by with home delivery from restaurants and occasional dine outs.

***

Time went on. I began to feel restless. I craved my beloved Bengali cuisine, while Priya was content savouring various vegetarian dishes from around the world.

I finally had to pull out my long-kept secret weapon, my cooking knowledge. Being away from home since graduation had forced me to learn how to cook. Priya on the other hand, had the privilege of having home cooked food for most of her life.

I saw this as an opportunity to establish the dominance of Bengali cuisine in our household.

I started to plot my diplomatic moves to get Priya on board.

"You know, I'm really tired of eating restaurant food," I shared my plea with Priya.

"Yes, finding a cook who can make Indian food here is impossible," she replied, echoing my concern.

"No worries, I can cook for us," I assured her.

"No, no, you don't need to do that. Just share the recipes with me, and I'll handle it," Priya stepped up.

"How can you? You just enrolled in K-language classes, and on top of that, you joined a non-profit organization here," I tried to make sure my compassion was registered.

"Yes, that's true…" Priya made a thoughtful U-turn.

That was a flag. My effort to show compassion was backfiring on me. Priya took me literally. She was backing out.

I had to change my tact. I decided to use the words that would make Priya act immediately.

"I don't think you can even do it. Making Bengali food is not that easy, a recipe alone cannot save your day. You need to get into the spirit of it," I said, letting the weight of my words sink in.

"What do you mean I can't keep up?" Priya shot back, her eyes flashing with steely determination. "I'll show you what I can do."

I let out a secret sigh of relief, my tactfully chosen words did their job.

The project began the following weekend. I was the expert and Priya, the apprentice.

To my relief, Priya picked up things quickly. But I still felt she was struggling with the two most important characteristics of a Bengali meal.

These two are…

First, in Bengali dishes, potato is indispensable. It becomes the hero in some dishes but for other dishes it must be there in a supporting role.

Second, the order of serving dishes in a meal. She struggled a bit to understand which dishes could qualify as openers, which ones should come in the middle order and finally which ones would be the tail enders.

Seeing her getting overwhelmed, I provided her with a few words of wisdom.

"For us, food isn't just fuel; it's an art form, a celebration to be savoured, not merely consumed to keep the engine running," I said.

Priya listened to me very carefully and smiled. Seemed like she finally got a hold on it.

And then, her cooking lessons were complete.

From thereon, the aroma of Bengali dishes started to fill our household.

I just sat back relaxed and offered her the critic's review.

How onions should be cut differently for various preparations, how spices should be crushed just so, and many more little details like that.

Priya was truly appreciative of my supreme knowledge in cooking.

Every dish she made felt like an ode to me.

***

Then came that fateful day—my parents arrived in K-land for a visit. My mother conducted a thorough audit of our place.

She had two questions. Would she be able to watch her Bengali soaps from here, and what would the food arrangements be?

The first one had already been settled. So, the point of contention was the second one.

Then she saw Priya cooking Bengali dishes. She was nearly in tears.

Every day right after lunch and dinner, she would call her entire contact list, proudly boasting about how well her 'South Indian' daughter-in-law had cooked Bengali dishes at home.

My father wasn't far behind.

In religious scriptures, they say jealousy is a sin. But seeing the halo around Priya, I couldn't resist the temptation to commit that very sin.

So one day, I decided to cook. I made four different dishes for them.

To this day, I regret that decision.

"Too spicy." … "A little burnt." … "It needed to be boiled a bit longer." … "The salt could've been a bit less." …

My mother's harsh criticism delivered a fatal blow to my cooking reputation with Priya.

"What are you saying Ma? He only taught me how to cook," Priya recounted respectfully.

"He taught you cooking! I am surprised, despite that you managed to learn to cook so well," Ma was sarcastic.

"He is just good in lecturing, when it comes to action, we all know how good he is, Baba added in.

Together, they ensured that the supreme image I had built in Priya's mind was shattered. They came, they saw, and they destroyed.

Priya and I never talked about it again.

ॐ

PRIYA'S PICK

Priya and I complemented each other quite well; her weaknesses happened to be my strengths and vice versa.

One glaring example of that was our sleeping schedule. After 9 PM, she would turn into a pumpkin—just like the one in the story of Cinderella—and wake up right at dawn.

I, on the other hand, was more like Bram Stoker's Count Dracula; my energy peaked at night. If it weren't for work obligations, I could easily stay up all night and sleep through the day.

Together, we perfectly exemplified '7/11's 24/7 service.

After moving to Gurgaon, there were hardly any movies we missed; multiplexes were our go-to spots.

But then, in K-land, our entire movie-watching ecosystem faced a major shift. The multiplexes here mainly played English films or K-movies. While they were good, they didn't satisfy our cravings for Bollywood.

Unfortunately, platforms like Netflix were late to arrive and quite restricted for a long time in K-land.

We relied on weekend DVD marathons to get our fix. Watching the same movies time and again beyond a point became little monotonous.

Determined to find a solution, Priya, with her resourcefulness, discovered a few websites streaming Indian movies. We hit the jackpot!

Friday nights transformed into movie nights as we turned our living area into a mini theater, exclusively for Priya and me.

During the week, she would thoroughly research the available movies, delving into everything from the cast to the synopsis, popular and critics reviews, and star ratings.

On a Friday night, at exactly 8 PM, the process would begin. Priya would share her recommendations.

The lights would be dimmed. We would settle on our four-seater sofa. The streaming of Priya's 'Pick of the Week' would begin.

'Smoking is Injurious to Health' … we would sail through the introductory acknowledgments and credits. Just as the film began, the screen would freeze. Priya would hit the pause button, turn on one light, and get up.

"Would you like to munch on something?" Before I could respond, she was already up and opening the fridge.

She would return with some munchies and soda, and we'd resume the movie. Just as we started scene two, the screen would freeze again. Priya would get up and head to the washroom.

"Why can't you finish everything before the movie?" I would complain.

"Nature's call can't be pre-planned," she would counter.

Priya would return in a while, seemingly all set and comfortable. We would resume the movie.

Suddenly I would feel a push. I would be dislodged from the sofa. The gentle hum of Priya's soft snoring would announce her departure from the real world to a dreamy one.

At its core, I always found it an interesting situation.

Together, we'd revel in our fantasies, me in the world of movies, and her in the realm of dreams.

I've always believed it's a carefully thought-out process by Priya. Through her weeklong research, she was producing her own Friday release.

No, not for OTTs or multiplexes, but for an exclusive screening in her dream. I would be left stranded on the sidelines with nothing but munchies and sodas, only to watch Priya's pick.

ॐ

THE TRAVEL TREPIDATION

I used to love traveling before marriage, but soon after our move to K-land, my interest waned.

I found myself enjoying staying at home more and was okay with only the occasional outing in the city.

One might wonder why. The answer lies in the very purpose of travel.

We generally travel to escape the hustle and bustle of daily life and take a break from work. However, my first travel experience with Priya in K-land complicated this notion.

We wanted to explore K-land beyond the city we were living in and take in the beauty of this scenic country.

"A long holiday is coming up next month," I said as I freshened up after returning from work.

"Yes, I know! They announced it in my K-language class. It's their annual Thanksgiving festival!" Priya replied excitedly.

It would be our first long holiday in K-land.

"But I'm not sure if my nonprofit organization will stop during the holidays," her tone shifted from excitement to concern.

"Yeah, they will. These are national holidays," I assured her.

Priya then got busy with her phone, and I wasn't sure if she even heard my last sentence.

At the dinner table, Priya looked quite happy, as if she had found all the clarifications she was looking for.

"Let's go somewhere," I suggested—an idea that would change my life forever.

"Yes!" Priya exclaimed, her enthusiasm soaring.

Unlike our escape to Africa, this time she eagerly volunteered to plan everything herself.

She plunged into research on every possible travel destination.

After careful consideration, she meticulously shortlisted our options.

Each place had its own unique attractions, and Priya thoughtfully highlighted the ones most meaningful to us and summarized them.

As much as Priya wanted full control of the travel plan, her collaborative nature led her to include me in the process.

So, she kicked things off with organized 'planning meetings'. We went through a series of meetings to zero down on the destination.

One might wonder if there were many deliberations between Priya and me.

I wish that were the case—then I could have curtailed the flow of thought by saying yes to the first suggestion she made.

It was Priya, debating options, based on their individual merit, with herself. I was simply her sounding board.

She was filled with an unimaginable amount of energy. She started to defy her usual 9 PM cutoff, letting our meetings run past midnight until I'd finally beg for some sleep.

The tough taskmaster in her would grant my request only once she was satisfied with the meeting's outcome.

For the first time, I realized that being a sounding board isn't easy. The constant vibrations of sound do take a toll on the board.

After countless rounds of meetings stretching across days and weekends, Priya finally zeroed in on a destination.

I felt a mix of relief and exhaustion—like a big project had finally wrapped up.

But my relief was short lived. Priya dragged me to the next stage. She wanted to finalize the logistics. The search for hotels, train and car bookings, discounts, special privileges, and more were all on the agenda.

Then came another round of meetings focused on optimizing these logistics. We went through the same process, but this time Priya's scenarios and possibilities seemed even more misaligned from the start.

The sounding board was crying out for help.

Finally, it all came to a close. Priya had a plan.

Seeing her sorting out the destination and logistics, I sprang into action. I was desperate for closure.

"Let me start booking," I said eagerly to Priya.

"How can we?" she asked, looking surprised.

"What do you mean?" I was puzzled.

"We still need to finalize our budget," she replied, sounding offended by my apparent carelessness.

"What?" I struggled to grasp her point. She had already finalized the transportation and secured hotel deals. We just needed to add them up.

"What, 'what'?" Priya sounded irritated.

"We still need to account for our expenses for my travel clothes, the entry fees to the exhibitions..." she rambled.

I was in shock. My head started to spin. To me, it was a grave warning of yet another round of meetings.

At the end of it all, there was only the 'sound'—the 'board' was on the verge of obliteration.

Even in that state, I somehow managed to close it all out with a few clicks on the internet. We were all set. Or at least, that's what I thought.

Priya was relentless. In the days leading up to our trip, she kept me awake, listing everything we must carry. The dresses for different occasions, her train attire, her walking-around outfits...

On the other hand, a sleep-deprived me, exhausted from this prolonged planning, was simply counting the days. Balancing work at the office and at home, the dual responsibilities were taking a serious toll on me.

*****

Finally, the big day came. I was fast asleep. Priya hurried me to get up. It was 5 AM.

"Our train is at nine, and the station is just fifteen minutes away. There are no check-in formalities to hold us up," I reasoned, hoping for another hour of sleep.

Priya didn't seem to have slept at all. She had shut herself in the other room, busy packing. "Please remind me of the essentials we should carry," she asked.

"The train tickets, hotel booking confirmations, cellphones, chargers, clothes…" I mumbled the usual list we'd rehearsed countless times.

"Okay, we're all set." She disappeared into the bathroom.

At 6 AM, she woke me up again. She had already showered and put on her travel outfit. She looked all set.

"Please go get ready, or we'll be late!" she urged.

By 6:30, I was ready, sitting on the sofa and fiddling with my phone while Priya walked back and forth between the rooms, gathering the last-minute essentials.

'Ting tong!' The doorbell rang. It was 7 AM, our ride to the station was there. The driver came up to inform us.

I found Priya in the second room, looking frazzled.

"What happened?" I asked, sensing her stress.

"Could you help me zip up the suitcase?" she replied, frustration evident in her voice.

The big black suitcase lying on the floor was about to burst at the seams, as if it were carrying an eight-month-old baby.

I felt a pang of sympathy for her; she must have stayed up the whole night trying to fit everything into one suitcase.

"Sure! You go ahead and get ready; our ride is here," I gently kissed her forehead, showering my appreciation for her humongous effort.

"I'm ready, just give me five minutes. Please zip up the suitcase," she said, disappearing into our bedroom.

With a deep breath, I tackled the suitcase. After a Herculean effort, I finally managed to zip it up without breaking the zip.

Half an hour had passed, and Priya was still missing, locked in our bedroom.

"Priya! Let's go!" I knocked on the door.

"Yes, just five more minutes!" she called back.

Meanwhile, the driver's patience was wearing thin. He switched from physical visits to phone calls, his once polite tone now tinged with annoyance.

Finally, the door opened, and Priya emerged. "How am I looking?"

I took a closer look, struggling to figure out what had changed in her look since 6 AM.

"You look just fine," I said, deciding to play it safe.

"Could you please bring the bags out?" she asked, a hint of urgency in her voice.

"The bags?" I was shocked.

"The other suitcases and our backpacks are on the other side of the cot. They were easy to miss. Please line them up here and ask the driver to pick them up," she instructed before disappearing back into the bedroom again.

I anxiously rushed into the second room, and there they were, just as she said, on the other side of the cot. And here I was, praising her for her packing efficiency.

"Priya, do we really need this much luggage?" I exclaimed in disbelief.

"Why not? We're not traveling by air, so there's no restriction, right?" She enlightened me as she finally walked out the main door of our apartment.

I had no courage left to call the driver. I'd heard terrifying stories about the angry drivers in K-land. I love living.

I took each piece of luggage down to the car one by one, and we finally set off at 8:30.

The rest of the trip was a blur. I slept through the train journey, dozed off in the car, and barely registered our time at the hotel.

I walked around the tourist spots like a zombie, holding Priya's hand for support. The long weeks of planning had finally caught up with me.

***

To this day, I don't remember how we returned home with all that luggage. But that trip marked a turning point in my life. My home, sweet home, became my sanctuary, and I realized just how much I cherished it.

ॐ

AN (IN)LAWFUL VISIT

It was a Sunday, and Priya and I were lounging in our living room, enjoying the leisurely pace of the day.

"They've finalized their travel plans," Priya announced.

My blood pressure shot up. I was still recovering from the exhaustion of our last trip.

"What happened? Say something," Priya poked me.

"Tr…rr…avel?" I stammered, my mind racing.

"Yes! Appa messaged you, right?" she asked, her excitement evident.

"Oh! That!" I sighed with relief.

"Yes, yes, of course! When are they coming?" I tried to mask my exhaustion with excitement.

"First week of next month," Priya confirmed.

"So, another three weeks," I calculated, trying to keep track. For some reason, this sudden announcement threw me off a bit.

"Yes!" Priya's eyes sparkled. This would be their first visit to K-land.

***

The big day finally arrived, and Priya and I headed to the city airport to pick them up. After the usual round of greetings, we boarded a cab and headed home.

In the cab, Appa couldn't stop talking about his efforts to secure the visa and flight bookings relaying how it all came together for a smooth arrival in K-Land. Oddly, he didn't mention a word about the flight experience itself. Meanwhile, Priya and her mother were engaged in a hushed conversation about topics that went over my head.

Before we knew it, the 45-minute journey was over.

"Wow! You have a lovely villa," Appa remarked as he stepped inside the house.

"It's all him," Priya said, giving me all the credit. I felt a swell of pride, but it was short-lived.

"But you made it a home; you're the one at the helm after all," Priya's mother said, looking at her daughter.

"Agh! She is so miserly with compliments for anyone outside her family," I whispered to Priya, who turned a shade of red.

"You guys change and freshen up; I'll make some tea," Priya said, expertly shifting the topic.

I showed them to their room—our second bedroom, which Priya had arranged neatly for their stay.

"So, how is your work?" Appa asked as we all settled around the center table, to enjoy a cup of tea.

"All good, Appa," I replied.

"I'd really like to understand your business operations this time since we'll be spending a lot of time together," Appa added.

I groaned inwardly. I was not looking forward to it.

Work is painful as it is, and home is my sanctuary. These are two distinct worlds that shouldn't collide. Priya often encouraged me to invite colleagues over, but I always found a way to sabotage those ideas.

"I'm sure you have some business plans. What kind of targets are you working towards?" Appa continued, his curiosity evident.

"Yes, Appa. We have some ambitious goals this year," I replied.

"So how was your flight?" I tried to shift the topic.

"Oh, as usual. You know we always travel in Business Class. Your Appa always keeps me in comfort and luxury," Priya's mother replied, her pride shining through.

Appa was listening to this with a smile.

"So, about your targets..." he returned to his original question.

I was amazed by his perseverance on that topic.

But my anxiety was rising. The worlds I had carefully kept separate for so long were about to collide, and I knew that could only bring destruction- destruction of my happy, peaceful home time.

"Sorry, Appa, I have to take this call," I said, glancing at my phone with feigned urgency before retreating to the bedroom. My last-ditch effort to sideline the topic.

Priya followed me a few minutes later.

"What's wrong with you? Why are you avoiding them?"

"I know there was no call; you just made an excuse to escape," she said, sounding unhappy.

I had to stop fiddling with my phone.

"Priya, you know my theory of two worlds..." I said.

"Ah..." Priya's tone softened, turning sympathetic.

"You be with them; I'll manage," she assured me.

On that note, I returned to the living room. Appa and Amma were still sitting there sipping their tea. Priya was getting dinner ready.

"Sorry about that. I had to take that call," I said, settling back into my seat.

"No problem. I have also been through those days. I have had many such experiences," Appa said.

Before he could elaborate on his experiences… "Sorry, we could not attend Bharath's wedding. Priya showed me quite a few photos. How did it go?" I brought up Priya's cousin's wedding to divert the conversation from corporate life to a homely affair.

"All good, all good." Appa replied.

"Yes, it was a lovely wedding, but nothing compared to what we had done for our Priya," Amma said with pride.

"Amma, please join me in the kitchen," Priya called out to her mother.

"Yes, now going back to our topic," Appa resumed, just as Amma joined Priya in the kitchen. "You were saying you have some ambitious goals…" The corporate interview was back on track.

"Yes Appa," I said, resigning myself to the inevitable. "The way our goals are assigned…"

"Gentlemen, please come to the table. Dinner is ready!" she announced, looking more proactive than usual.

I had a narrow escape.

***

"I wish I had the power of Superman," I sighed

She looked at me quizzically as she climbed into bed.

"To prevent the worlds from colliding," I added.

Priya caressed my head gently.

"Please bear with him. He still can't keep his corporate life behind, even after two years of retirement," she said soothingly.

"But how can we stop him from doing shop talk?" I was feeling desperate.

"You might want to find some topics of common interest," Priya suggested gently.

"What are his interests?" I asked, eager to know.

"Hmm, let's see," Priya pondered. "He likes movies, he likes cricket…"

Before she could finish the list, she dozed off.

Since India was not playing any international match around that time, my only option was to keep him busy with movies.

I started planning. First, I made a mental calculation of how much time I needed to spend with them. I excluded my office hours, my 'getting ready' time, and my 'freshening up' time.

This significantly lightened the load. Their one-month stay had boiled down to only four weekends (eight days) and a few hours a day during the week, amounting to another forty-eight or so hours.

"I can manage that," I told myself. A straight 70% reduction made me feel comfortable. Plus, there would be sightseeing and dining out, further reducing the chance of any shop talk with him. Feeling super happy with that thought, I drifted off to sleep.

On my way to work the following morning, I began crafting a mental list of TV shows and movie DVDs I wanted to focus on. The criteria for selection were straightforward: they had to be reasonably long and gripping. I couldn't afford to have slow or uninteresting shows and movies that might divert his attention or lead to awkward conversations about work.

I thought of action-packed thrillers, engaging dramas, and perhaps a few classic comedies that would keep him entertained. My goal was to ensure that our time together would be enjoyable and distraction-free, steering clear of any corporate talk.

Every evening after I returned from work, we'd engage in some casual chit-chat, and then I'd quietly slip in a DVD for us all to enjoy.

Everything was falling into place. We became good friends, and I began to enjoy the time we spent together.

In the meantime, Priya was happily indulging in her mother's home-cooked meals. Bengali cuisine had taken a backseat, while Tamil dishes took over the dining table.

And while I was at work, Priya would take them out to explore the city. She even took a break from her language classes and nonprofit work during their stay.

Everything was going perfectly according to plan, filled with laughter, good food, and plenty of memorable moments.

***

Then came that fateful Sunday morning, probably the third one during their stay. While an early riser back home, Appa had let himself slide into a relaxed routine while on holiday. But for some reason, he decided to get up early that day.

"Wake up! Appa wants to go out for a walk with you," Priya said, pulling me from the depths of my weekend slumber.

"What?" I mumbled, trying to process her words.

"A walk! And this early? What's going on?" I was suspicious, my mind racing with scenarios.

"I don't know! He just said he wanted to go out for a walk with you. Get up; I'm making your tea," she replied, clearly limited in her information, before disappearing into the kitchen.

I sighed inwardly, aware that I had little choice in the matter. Appa was up and ready, and there was no way I could dodge this. I hauled myself out of bed and freshened up.

"We can have our morning tea outside," Appa said firmly, dismissing any notion of wasting time. Priya shot me a helpless look, clearly caught in the middle.

Just then, her mother emerged from our little Puja room and smeared some ashes on my forehead, a traditional gesture. I didn't quite understand why this was done before what seemed like a casual walk. A sense of unease started to creep in, and I began to feel paranoid.

As we stepped out into the street, Appa suggested, "Let's go somewhere we can sit and talk in peace over a cup of coffee."

My heart began to race. The way he said it made me think there was more to this walk than just casual conversation.

I flagged down a cab and told the driver to take us to the park, about 15 minutes away. As he drove, my mind was in overdrive. My paranoia was escalating, each passing moment adding to the unease gnawing at me.

Appa seemed lost in his own world, humming a bhajan with his eyes closed, comfortably leaning back on the seat.

To distract myself, I began counting bananas in my head… "One banana, two bananas…" After what felt like counting hundreds of them, we finally reached our destination.

Appa finally opened his eyes as I collected the payment receipt from the driver. We entered the park.

"Let's pick up our coffee from there," I told Appa, pointing to the coffee stall at the far end of the park.

"Sounds good," he confirmed.

We strolled through the park and grabbed our coffee.

"Let's sit there," Appa said, gesturing to a bench under a tree. The park was nearly empty; it was only half past seven. As we settled in, he slipped into a trance, seemingly lost in thought.

Multiple possibilities raced through my mind. "What could this be about?" I kept wondering, glancing at him occasionally.

In the stillness of the park, the only sound I could hear was the quiet sip of Appa's coffee.

"So…" He finally broke his silence.

"You know it's almost two years since you two got married," he continued. "Especially considering you both got married a little later than is usual in our culture." His tone was advisory, almost paternal.

I felt another wave of unease wash over me. I wasn't sure how to respond, and my surprise must have been evident on my face. But Appa, lost in his own world, completely missed my reaction, his eyes still closed as he sipped his coffee.

"I'm not in favour of this generation's penchant for late marriages. You two should have made the decision much earlier," he declared.

My anxiety about not knowing where he was going with this completely overshadowed the irony I saw in his statement.

"The more you delay from here, the more complicated it could be," he said.

"Delay… Complication…" I started scratching my head, trying to figure out the context.

I thought that with marriage, Priya and I had left all these terms behind.

"You need to start your family planning," he concluded.

I felt like a massive explosion had just gone off inside my head. The ringing in my ears was intense, and my stomach felt hollow. If we weren't already sitting, I would have collapsed to the ground.

"Family planning?… All my privileges would be stripped away. I still need all the baby privileges… How can I become a parent?" These thoughts spiralled through my mind, freaking me out from the inside.

Now, Appa's eyes were fixed on me. He was waiting for my response.

I was scrambling for an answer when, in that very moment, I heard a divine voice in my ear.

"Yes, I agree. Priya and I will discuss this," I said, trying to keep my voice steady.

"I'm glad to see you understand my point. Anyway, discuss this with Priya and mull it over," he replied, satisfaction gleaming in his eyes. After some small talk, we took a cab back home.

The funny side of it all—I had left home a paranoid wreck, only to return a bundle of stress and anxiety.

What would Priya think about Appa's advice, I wondered.

"How did it go?" Priya asked as I came out of the washroom.

Before giving her a full download, I hesitated.

"Just some fatherly advice," I said with a smile.

ಶ್ರೀ

SHE IS MY GIRL

I was travelling for work. I was in the middle of a meeting, when I received a sudden message from Priya. She asked me to call her back when I got free.

It was quite unusual of her. She never texts or calls me during my work hours. She was alone in a foreign land at that time, and this unexpected action of hers threw me off.

I was completely distracted. All I wanted was to wrap up the meeting quickly so I could call her back.

Finally, after about an hour, I got a brief 15-minute window. I hurriedly stepped out and found a cozy corner next to a Starbucks outside.

Without any delay I dialed her number. My legs were shaking with anxiety.

"We did it!" she exclaimed, her voice filled with excitement.

"Ani… I'm pregnant," she added, the words sinking in slowly.

"What happened? Say something…" she urged. I was spellbound, not knowing how to react.

I couldn't find the words to describe my own feelings, especially over the phone.

"Congratulations, baby…" Somehow, I managed to get those two words to travel over the phone to the most special person in my life.

"Aren't you happy?" she asked, her voice tinged with concern.

"Of course I am, I just don't know how to describe my feelings," I clarified, not wanting Priya to misunderstand my slow reaction on the phone.

"Okay, go back to your meetings now. We'll talk more tonight," she said before disconnecting the call.

I stood there for a while. I simply could not understand how I was feeling. I was going to be a father.

I was late for the next meeting. If it hadn't been for my assistant's proactiveness in finding me, I might have stood there all day, trying to analyze my emotions.

During the rest of the meetings, I found myself absent, observing people's lips moving up and down, but my mind was elsewhere.

Finally, the day came to an end. I rushed back to my hotel. I dialled Priya's number.

She really made it easy for me. Priya talked about the tests she had done, what the reports said, and what the doctor advised. With all the medical terms and doctors' recommendations, the whole situation started to feel more like a project to me.

Priya seemed to be in full control. Suddenly, the feelings that had troubled me throughout the day seemed to vanish.

Upon my return, I began to feel the ticking of the clock. Priya spared me from the proverbial 'pregnancy tantrums'. Both she and the baby were incredibly kind to me.

With the news of Priya's pregnancy, both our parents went ecstatic.

Seeing their eagerness to visit Priya, I realized I needed to find another place. The family was clearly in expansion mode.

***

Then came the big day. It was a Sunday morning when Priya woke me up, her tone filled with urgency.

"We need to go to the hospital," she said.

"Right now!!!" she followed up, leaving no room for any further delay.

I woke up the whole house.

We had just moved into a four-bedroom place, with each set of parents occupying one room. The other room that Priya had thoughtfully decorated for our soon-to-arrive little one, was ready.

Priya and I sat in our SUV, with both mothers joining us. Our fathers were asked to follow in a cab.

As I saw Priya lying in the bed of the private room, those lost feelings began to resurface.

I realized then what had been bothering me all along. I never doubted that Priya would be an amazing mother, but me- could I do a good job as a father?

The only example I had in front of me was my own father. That made things quite complicated.

The compromises, the sacrifices, the patience—was I truly ready for any of it? I didn't even know how to hold that tiny life that was soon to arrive.

I started to freak out. Priya's contractions began.

I was still overwhelmed, but now for a different reason—I didn't want a single thing to go wrong.

The doctor arrived, and the procedures began. Then, a loud scream filled the room, and in that moment, a flood of relief washed over both Priya and me.

Without any delay, I immediately texted our anxious parents. They were not allowed to enter the delivery room.

"She has arrived, her name is Aniya," the text read.

***

Our parents stayed back for a few more weeks. A few rituals took place.

Once they left and our initial excitement began to settle down, I started to notice the changes.

Aniya was becoming increasingly demanding.

The first casualty was my sleeping schedule. Aniya dictated when we could sleep and when we had to stay awake to tend to her needs. It became clear that the rigid hours and minutes humanity had established held no sway in her decision-making.

"Ani, wake up! We need to change her diaper," Priya would say, rousing me at ungodly hours while Aniya screamed at the top of her lungs.

My sleep cycle was completely derailed, leading me to do things I'd never imagined, napping at work, dozing off on the living room sofa, and dealing with messy diapers.

Then came the next phase. I was banished from our bedroom. The princess needed calm and comfort.

"Ani, you may want to sleep in the other room, that way Aniya gets her sleep uninterrupted," Priya suggested one morning, her voice filled with concern.

"She has her own room… you spent so much… why can't she sleep there?" I tried to reason it out. But Priya was adamant. She made this a non-negotiable verdict. "Aniya First".

There came the next casualty, I had to move to another room.

My access to the bedroom, that was once known to be ours, became time bound.

To enter, I had to send a WhatsApp message to Priya for a pre-approval request. Aniya's comfort around any such visit decided the fate of such requests.

I couldn't even recognize our house anymore. The elegant furniture that adorned the place when we moved in had been pushed aside.

Everything was baby proofed. A playpen replaced all the furniture in the living room. Only the sofa was spared.

The vibrant colors of toys and baby gear started to dominate every corner of our house. Who knew when and where our Princess would decide to pay a surprise visit.

We did not want to upset her.

Our once stylish and modern home had transformed into a mini nursery. Chaos took over the peace and the structure of our life.

Then I saw my worst nightmare coming true. Priya's attitude towards me started to change completely. I was replaced.

Aniya was now everything to her—her going-out buddy, her playmate, her source of joy.

Like a forgotten piece of furniture, I just stayed there and watched.

Without Aniya's acceptance nothing would move.

I started to feel guilty for inadvertently disturbing the peace Aniya demanded.

My WhatsApp status changed to 'No calls, text only'. I began to forget the ringtone of my phone as it remained perpetually on silent mode.

Whenever I got some moments with Priya, the tiniest noise from the Princess would make her dump me and run, leaving me all alone.

Our once peaceful home had turned into a fortress under siege, with the Princess holding all the power.

Basic human rights had been suspended, and the kingdom revolved entirely around her commands.

***

A year passed like that. Aniya learned to walk, and she was starting to talk. I saw an opportunity. I made my move.

I increased my face time with her. We played together, we watched nursery rhymes together. I started to gain her acceptance.

With time, Aniya and I grew closer and closer. I had to make a few sacrifices and compromises in the process to earn her trust.

I gave up my weekend TV time, my sofa time. I even spent more time in the kitchen preparing foods she liked. Slowly, I realized that I didn't start off too badly as a father after all.

Although the most exciting part came later.

Priya started becoming jealous. Aniya was becoming more of a Father's girl.

After nine months, followed by countless sleepless nights, she wanted more of her.

But who in the universe can conquer the bond between a father and daughter?

She's still sulking, and I'm enjoying every moment of it.

ೲೱೲ

To be continued…

www.ingramcontent.com/pod-product-compliance
Lightning Source LLC
Chambersburg PA
CBHW061440160726
47995CB00003B/970